For **Orian**
love from
Sam Williams x

For my family
Matt Hunt

First published in Great Britain
in 2019 by Boxer Books Limited.
www.boxerbooks.com
Boxer® is a registered trademark
of Boxer Books Limited.

The text is set in Verveine
ISBN 978-1-912757-13-8

1 3 5 7 9 10 8 6 4 2

Printed in China
All of our papers are sourced from managed forests
and renewable resources.

HOW ABOUT A NIGHT OUT?

by
Sam
Williams

Illustrated
by
Matt Hunt

Boxer
Books

Lap cats are lazy cats

Who only sleep on hallway mats.

But city cats, like city lights,

How about a night out?

A walk about?

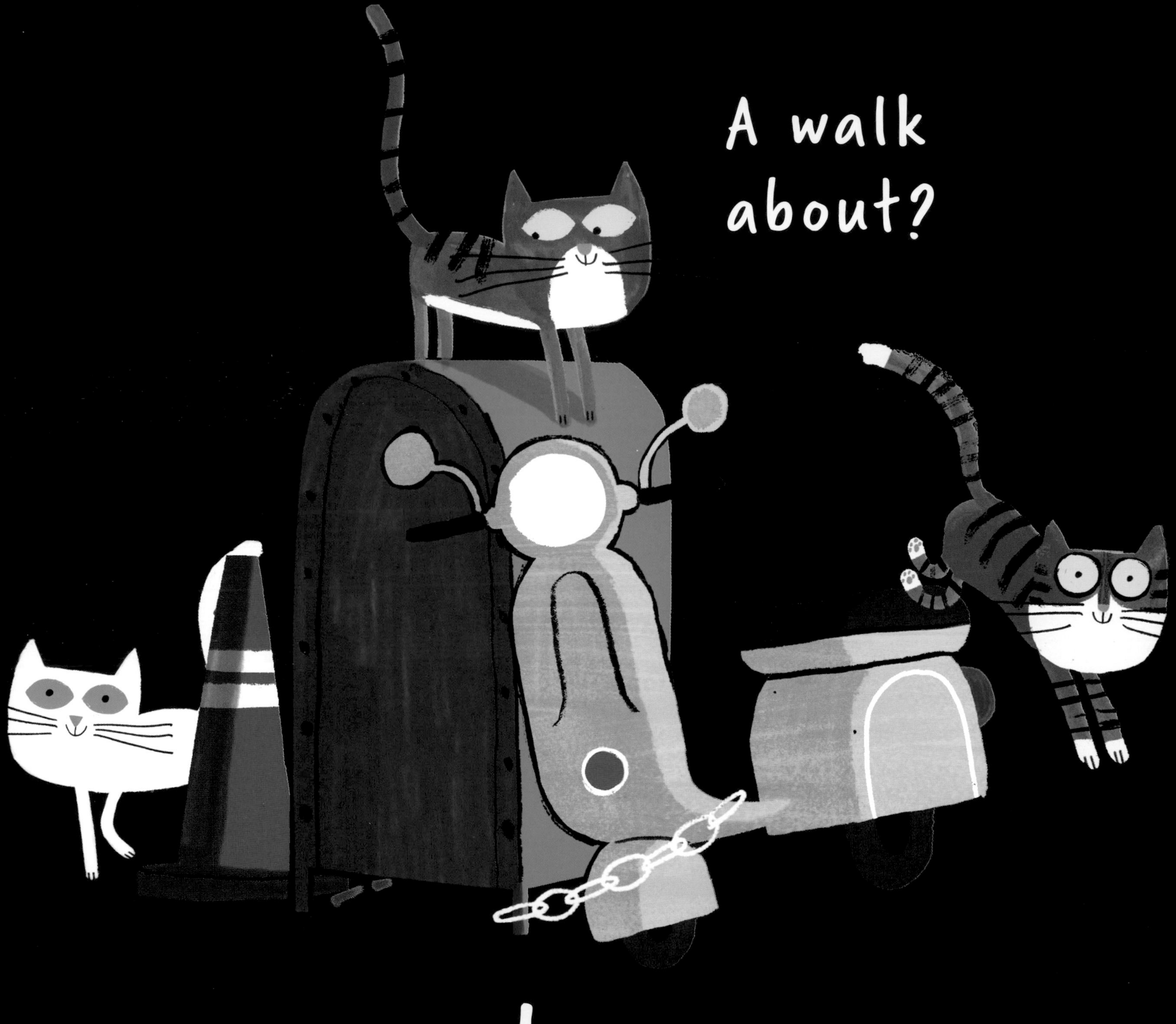

A **prowl** about?

Perhaps there'll
be an owl about?
Hooting about . . .

whoooo
knows
what!

on the roundabout.

We'll **SWOON** to the moon if the moon is out.

We'll have a night
to **sing** about.

Miaowton

Karaoke

We'll catercall upon the wall

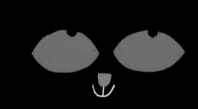

And never worry if we fall.

We'll **scare** the birds
that roost about.

We'll see the cars
go in and out.
And watch the people
move about . . .

And see them put
the rubbish out.

We'll hear the babies
cry and shout
And then we'll see
the sun come out.

And all too soon
there is no moon . . .

For when
it's morning
in the city . . .